This book belongs to…

_____

JUNGLE TALES
Hippo's Holiday

Written by Ronne Randall
Illustrated by Jacqueline East

Bright ☆ Sparks

It was a warm, sunny morning in the jungle.

"A perfect time for a nice, long, relaxing wallow," thought Howard Hippo.

Wallowing in the river was Howard's favourite thing to do.

He found a nice, cool, muddy spot and settled in. Howard was just drifting off into a delightful daydream, when…

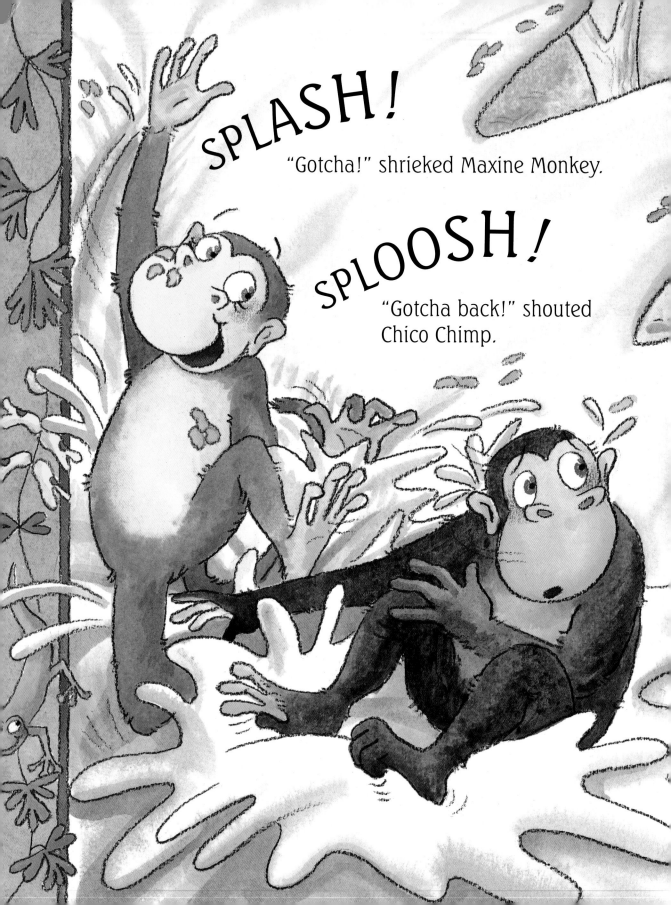

"Can't you monkeys and chimps play somewhere else?" Howard grumbled. "I'm wallowing here!"

"Oops! Sorry, Howard," Maxine apologised. "We'll move further down the river." But it was too late. Howard's morning wallow was ruined.

That afternoon, as the hot sun beat down on his back, Howard slithered into the river to cool off.

"Aaah," he breathed, as the cool water soaked his bottom. "This is soooo lovely."

"Yoo-hoo!
Howard!"

called Penelope Parrot. "I've just
learned to do a double-rollover-loop-the-loop!
Want to see?"

"Sure, Penelope," sighed Howard. It didn't look as if he was going to have a chance to relax this afternoon, either!

The next morning, Howard's cousin, Hilary, came to visit.

"You look exhausted, Howard," she said.

"That's because I never have a chance to relax and wallow any more," said Howard.

"What you need is a holiday," said Hilary. "I'm leaving for Hippo Hollow this afternoon. Why don't you come with me?"

"That sounds like a good idea!" said Howard.

As the two hippos trundled through the jungle, Hilary told Howard about Hippo Hollow.

"You'll love it," she said. "There's so much mud!"

Howard saw himself relaxing in a deep, cool mud bath.

"And there are streams and waterfalls!" continued Hilary.

Howard imagined himself having lots of cool showers.

"And everyone has lots and lots of FUN!" finished Hilary.

Howard thought about playing games with new hippo friends.

Later that day, Howard and Hilary arrived at Hippo Hollow. It was even more beautiful than Howard had imagined. "It's like a dream come true!" he exclaimed.

"And it looks like we've arrived just in time!" said Hilary.

"In time for what?" asked Howard. "A nice, relaxing mud bath?"

"No, silly!" laughed Hilary. "Hippo-robics!"

A sleek-looking hippo was galloping towards the stream, with lots of other hippos following her.

"Let's get moving, everyone!" she shouted, as they all charged into the stream.

"Come on, Howard," said Hilary. "Don't be a party pooper on the first day of your holiday!"

Howard had no choice but to join in.

"Kick, two, three, four! Kick two, three, four!" shouted the instructor.

Howard did his best and kicked with all the others.

"Surely everyone will want a nice, long rest after all this exercise?" he thought.

But he was wrong! After a quick shower in the waterfall, everyone rushed off to play Volley-Melon and Hilary wanted Howard in her team.

Howard finally did get to have a rest after
lunch – but not for long!

"You're looking much more relaxed, Howard," Hilary called, as she led her junior swimming class right past him. "This holiday was just what you needed, wasn't it?"

"Er… I guess so," Howard replied, weakly.

After his busy day, Howard was hoping for an early night. He was just getting settled, when he heard Hilary.

"Come on, Howard!" she bellowed. "It's time for the Hippo-Hooray Cabaret! You don't want to miss this!"

"They're good, aren't they?" said Hilary,
as they watched the cabaret dancers.

"Oh – YAWN – wonderful," sighed Howard.
He could barely keep his eyes open.

The next morning, Howard was just sliding into the river, when he heard Hilary calling.

"Is it time for Hippo-robics again?" he asked.

"Oh, no," said Hilary. "Lots of good, fresh air is what you need. So we're going on a hike!"

Howard huffed and puffed all through the hot, exhausting hike. "I hope I can have a nice cool bath when this is all over," he thought.

Howard got his wish. But, as he was soaking his sore muscles, Hilary came by for a chat.

"The hike was fun, wasn't it?" she said.

"Oh yes," said Howard. "In fact, I enjoyed it so much, that I've decided to go on another one!"

"Really?" said Hilary. "That's great! Where are you hiking to?"

"Home!" said Howard. "I'm going back home, where I can have a REAL holiday — with no Hippo-robics, no Volley-Melon games, no cabarets and no one to stop me from wallowing as long as I like!"

And that's just what Howard did!

The
End